In the Shadows Where the Boys Used to Play

Paul Carro

ISBN: 978-1-7350701-9-3

Cover by Wendy Saber Core

CONTENTS

IN THE SHADOWS WHERE THE BOYS USED TO PLAY

All land was God's land, Father Parnell often thought, but he struggled to remember that while riding shotgun up a Romanian mountain in a jeep long past its expiration and exploration date. A scruffy man who some might describe as a member of the unwashed masses manned the wheel. The driver was an affable sort at the start of their trip, but his antics behind the wheel while ascending the mountain caused Parnell to consider whether an exorcism was in order.

"There are other gears, you know," Father Parnell said, hoping the man might take a hint.

"Only need the one."

Parnell looked to his right where the narrow dirt road absent guardrails dropped precipitously. There would be no surviving such a fall were they to crash. "You ever lose anyone making this drive?"

"Oh yes," the man said.

Sebastian was the driver's name. Parnell noted it because he wished to know the name of the man who would likely kill him. The driver took the turns at dangerous speeds. After one such turn, Parnell attempted to make a cross over his chest. Before he could finish, the jeep hit a pothole, lifting the priest into the air. In the moment before the seatbelt took hold, Parnell expected to finally meet God in a more formal setting than his church back in Massachusetts.

Though the seatbelts saved both passengers, the cargo did not fare as well. A cord in the back snapped with a twang and his suitcase bounced around the jeep's back before flying over the cliff. Parnell caught a glimpse, but it was too late.

"My suitcase," he said. "We have to go back."

"It's gone now," Sebastian said as he continued speeding along the perilous road.

Near the mountain's top, the road widened, allowing them to put distance between the vehicle and the cliffs.

Unlike the dirt road, the long circular driveway to the church was paved. The priest felt the journey would have been smoother were the whole road made of asphalt, but paving all the way to the clouds would have been a monumental task. But then *God did work miracles,* Parnell thought. For example, he survived the trip.

The school came into view: a grand building with high arches reaching toward the heavens. The driveway was a cul-de-sac. It looped from where the priest stood and circled back to a spot further down the main road. Trees surrounded the orphanage, an endless forest vast as any ocean.

"You get out here," Sebastian said, skidding to a stop at the driveway's entrance.

Father Parnell waved away the resultant dust and looked from the man to the distant school. "It's rather far. Might I request you drive me to the school's entrance?"

"You might, but I will say no." The man made his own sign of the cross.

Eager to get out of the jeep in one piece, Parnell pushed it no further. He stepped from the vehicle, which roared off, using the mouth of the driveway as a turnaround. Without so much as a departing horn beep, the jeep vanished in a fresh dust cloud, racing down the mountain at the same unsafe speed it had ascended.

All Father Parnell's worldly possessions brought from the states lay scattered over the mountainside. Thankfully, his religious possessions remained safely in the small black satchel he held in his lap during the trip. He carried the small bag while climbing the driveway on foot.

The long walk allowed Parnell time to acquaint himself with the school's exterior. The church excelled at constructing buildings worthy of God's followers, and the school in the distance was no different. Impressive in both size and design, the orphanage sat so high on the mountain it could serve as a bridge to heaven.

A church was always the first building on any such campus. The school would sit behind that, as would a bell tower. Sure enough, well past the main building, a campanile rose higher than the main building. The brick tower was cylindrical but tapered at the top, where it housed a large bell. The way the tower peaked reminded Parnell of grain silos back in the states. Atop the campanile's roof rose a large cross, one of many topping different peaks of various buildings. From the priest's vantage point, he could only make out the top two floors of the tower. The balance of the campanile remained hidden behind the church.

The circular part of the tower below the bell had a series of large, square openings in place of windows. Such openings were designed to boost acoustics while also serving as a watchtower from which church elders could oversee children on the playground. Though unable to see a playground or dormitory from his vantage point, the priest knew they were behind the church. Sadly, many orphanages were cookie cutter designs—a social safety-net version of tract homes.

The church's three-tiered front featured a series of arches that evoked a sense of grandeur worthy of God. The building was a jewel nestled against the backdrop of the dense Romanian forest. *From God to God*, Parnell thought of the building in relation to its surroundings. Forest meeting sky was so beautiful it all but confirmed God's hand in creation. The church itself looked timeless and would have to be to survive centuries in such a remote area.

It was only when Parnell finally reached the end of the driveway that cracks in the building's façade appeared. Literally. Despite the stunning view from a distance, up close, the place appeared decrepit. What he thought were vines cradling one side of the school like ivy league colleges were branches of black mold, spread in a crystalline pattern. Like a dark hand trying to steal the building from the Lord.

Broken ceramic roof tiles littered the driveway near the main entrance. Parnell grunted. It was one thing to lack funds for proper maintenance, but to leave such a mess at the doorsteps of a church bordered on blasphemy. Parnell planned to take it up with the headmaster, but only after learning why he was called to such a remote school in the first place. The church hierarchy reached out to Parnell weeks earlier (a surprise, as he was unaware that they were aware of him).

Parnell was not one to question the church, so he made the trip as requested. Now he stood at the entrance to a school like many he taught at in the past. Still, the reason for his presence remained a mystery.

The church rose higher than its interconnected building to the left. A brick corridor lined with open-air arched windows connected the buildings. Any structure attached to a church usually served as staff living quarters. Combined, the interconnected building reminded Father Parnell of the Basilica of Sant'Apollinare in Italy. The priest had some experience with other religious institutions. A 'Southie' from New England, Parnell had traveled extensively with the church over the years.

Cracks lined the building's façade in spots not doused in mold. The condition of the school made little sense to Parnell. Boys' orphanages housed rebellious individuals who required structure and discipline. Surely, many earned punishment by the sheer nature of being boys. Giving them a bucket and brush would have solved two problems. Penance through paint. A clean school and a clean start for any offenders. One more thing for Parnell to suggest to the headmaster.

"Hello?" Parnell called out.

Silence greeted him, though a flash of movement caught his eye. Through one of the corridor arches stood a child, maybe twelve.

"You there boy, please direct me to the headmaster," Parnell called out only for the child to vanish.

There was no secondary entrance through which to enter the corridor other than through the church. That left the priest no avenue to pursue and scold the kid. But then Parnell was on foreign ground and was unsure of what language the boy understood. The church assured Parnell they were sending him to an English-speaking school, but sending him there for what? Parnell's frustration lay with the mystery of his mission, not with the antics of a frightened boy. He dismissed any plans to reprimand the child.

"Father Parnell?" A woman called out.

Parnell turned to find a nun standing in the open doorway of the church. Her habit was standard, her face less so. Bright with no hint of surly. Her smile was weary, but infectious. The nun did not wait for him to approach. She descended the stairs and greeted him with a handshake.

"You have me at a disadvantage sister..."

"Sister Camelia. Welcome to our school, Father Parnell."

"Thank you. If you would be so kind as to lead me to your headmaster, I have much to discuss. Starting with my need for accommodations and new clothes."

She turned and started back up the stairs, gesturing for the priest to follow. "Let me guess, a victim of Sebastian's driving?"

Parnell nodded. "Please tell me he does not drive the children into town in such a fashion."

"No, Sebastian has no affiliation with the church. The man is simply a mountain driver by occupation."

Parnell nodded. No need to complain about being dropped off at such a distance then. Parnell found himself full of complaints but did not wish to burden such a pleasant woman with topics best saved for the headmaster. They arrived at the top of the stairs.

"I urged one boy to direct me to the headmaster, but the youth ran away instead."

Sister Camelia turned back to the priest. "You saw one of the boys?"

"Yes," Parnell said.

"What did the child look like?"

"Truthfully? A shadow."

She nodded. "It would serve you well to note who it is you see and speak to."

"Why? Is there a troublemaker in your midst?"

"One. But you will meet him soon enough."

The pair stepped through the doorway into a church in frightful disrepair. Parnell fought the urge to gasp, once again saving his ire for the hierarchy. Did they send him to pitch in with repairs? Unlikely, Parnell had many skills, but building an ark or fixing broken pews was not among them. His skills were more idiosyncratic. Audio engineering, podcasting, things of that type.

Through teaching and podcasting (faith versus super-natural occurrences) Parnell developed a formal speaking style that he understood could put off some parishioners who wanted the local accent and occasional curse words. When preaching, Parnell could *pahk the cah* with the best of the Boston area congregants, but mostly his speech re-mained accent free. He hoped it would help him commu-nicate with the Romanian children.

The sister led them through the decayed interior. Yellow caution tape dangled like party streamers throughout the church. Multiple pews were sealed off by the tape. As much sunlight entered the church through holes in the ceiling as it did through the stained-glass windows. The former glory of the building remained but had long since lost any semblance of a safe refuge for pilgrims of faith.

Parnell fell a step behind the nun so hurried to catch up. She led him out a rear door into a vast courtyard bursting with weeds and scrub. The brown dried lot resembled those of churches in underprivileged cities in the states. The courtyard's condition seemed out of place against the backdrop of lush green forest in the distance.

A large wing not visible from the building's front ran the length of the courtyard alongside the playground. The playground was set in dirt, with a merry-go-round, see-saw, slide, and jungle gym. Tetherball poles sat three in a row. A wide-open lot past the poles probably served as a place to play soccer and other sports.

Clear windows lined the first and second stories of the building at equidistant intervals. Stained glass was reserved for the church and priest's quarters. There was more mold on the rear building than there was at the front of the orphanage. Dense patches of fungus emulated blots on Rorschach cards. One such pattern caught Parnell's eye.

High on the second story, an enormous mold patch had formed around two windows. The windows, though dirty, remained clear, which gave them the appearance of eyes set in a face. A horrendous face.

A patch below the "eyes" looked like a pig's snout. Directly below that, sat a wide grin of clenched teeth. The disturbing face appeared to have no lips. Not there would be lips. The whole thing was a pattern, not a painting. Still, the way the image came together was disturbing right down to what looked like tusks jutting from either side of a jaw. With minimal space between the window eyes, and the eaves, the face wore the roof as a cap. (The least foreboding thing about the image.)

Sunlight animated the windows, making it appear as if the building monitored the playground. Or maybe it watched the priest and nun. Absurd. Some people found Jesus's image in burnt toast, clouds, or even potato chips. Parnell never gave such accounts much thought other than believing someone needed God in their life and saw what they needed to see.

So why did the priest see something sinister in the patches of mold? A shiver ran through him, but he attributed it to moving from the sun to the shade. If the nun saw anything out of the ordinary, she did not let on.

"First floor serves as classrooms, the second floor is housing," Camelia said.

The sister remained in tour guide mode, seemingly oblivious to the hideous shape on the wall. It was only Parnell who failed the Rorschach test. He felt silly about it. A second batch of mold off to one side looked like a Manga character that many of his young parishioners might draw during Sunday school art classes. More than the imagined patterns, the building's overall condition disturbed the priest.

"Mold on living quarters? How is that allowed? Children deserve better."

"You are worried about the children?" the nun asked.

"Yes."

"That is why you are here."

"I do not understand, sister. The tour is much appreciated, but I need more answers than that. I do not understand my mission, nor the state of this decayed house of worship."

The church bell rang in the tower. Though it caught the priest off guard, the sound was too beautiful to frighten. The openings in the tower did their job, projecting the majestic chime not only across the courtyard but across the countryside. It was a sound that never grew old for Parnell. He loved every variation of every house of worship he ever visited. Its sound brought him peace. Even the shape on the wall appeared to change. At the very least, the building was no longer watching him and the nun, not that it ever was.

"When the bell rings, class is in session. I only ask that you observe rather than interact. I will reconvene with you when the period is over."

She gestured to an arched doorway where heavy oak doors sat closed. Parnell opened them and stepped inside. He looked back at the woman, curious, but did not wish to be late for class. He entered the dim corridor. Rooms lined both sides of the long hallway in a straight shot through the building.

There appeared to be no electricity, making it difficult to see. Random puddles of light leaked through windows on either side of the building and spilled into the hall wherever doors were open. Those random light shafts allowed him to navigate the corridor with caution. The lack of proper lighting illuminated the school's problem. The orphanage must have run out of funds. Was everything as simple as that?

Such a situation would explain why the church called him. Though nearing forty, Parnell long ago noticed how younger generations worshipped at the altar of the internet. For many years, it had become increasingly difficult to give young people a space where they could embrace their spiritual beliefs without being chastised for their reliance on technology.

Parnell took it upon himself to learn all the latest tech, and to stay up on trends so that he could pepper terms into his sermons that connected with the younger folks. His older congregants often scratched their heads over certain phrases or terms, but in those moments, Parnell shared a smile with the kids who understood.

They also enjoyed his podcast about the paranormal. And while he did not believe in every topic he covered, he felt it important to recognize that God reveals mysteries in His own time. Who was to say which ghostly events caught on camera were part of some miracle and which were not? Even aliens, if they existed, could be God's creations.

If the school was in financial trouble (and clearly it was), Parnell was the perfect one to run an online crowdfunding campaign. Based on the corridor's condition, fundraising could not come soon enough. Broken tiles lined the dust covered floor. An unpleasant stench filled the hallway.

Parnell took a moment to adjust to the gloom before advancing. Unsure of which classroom was occupied, he set out to check them all. Opening the nearest door revealed a room in disarray. The ceiling had partially collapsed. Through the broken ceiling, he glimpsed a wheelchair and medical bed on the second floor. He hoped there was more than one medical station on the compound because the one above was out of commission.

Where was the class sister Camelia instructed him to observe? A voice down the hall boomed like a church bell. No mistaking that it belonged to an authority figure. The headmaster? A teacher, at least. (Or professors, as they were called at orphanages.) The priest followed the voice to an open doorway. Once there, he entered and found a pristine classroom. Sunlight filled the room.

The classroom fell into a hush as the priest entered. All heads turned Parnell's way. Used to classrooms, Parnell did not feel self-conscious but did not wish to remain the focus of their attention, so he moved to the last row and took a seat. The seating was a traditional chair, desk combo, designed for mixed ages.

Orphanages could not plan course loads built around specific age groups, because the orphans arrived at different times, with different skill levels and ages. Classes had to adapt and teach the most students the most information they could. The boys in the class appeared to be between eleven and fourteen, a rare convergence of ages. Parnell settled into the too-small chair and waited for the teacher to continue his lecture.

"As I was saying, class, time is ethereal," the teacher said.

Parnell frowned. Ethereal? The man had used a college level word in the presence of children. Maybe this was an advanced class. The priest looked around to identify which textbook the students used but all the desks were empty. It was purely a lecture then.

None of the children wore the same outfits either. Their clothing varied wildly. That struck Parnell as odd, but based on the state of the building, maybe even clothing resources were scarce. *Or all the children lost their luggage on the way to school as well*, he thought, only half-joking.

With his back now turned to the class, the professor wrote on the chalkboard. Though the priest could not see the man's face, he had already studied the man's appearance. The professor sported a pencil-thin moustache straight from movies of a bygone era. His hair was slicked back and coiffed in a gentleman's part. He was tall in stature but trim in build and could have stepped off a 1940s movie screen.

Oddly enough, the man wore no religious vestments, choosing instead to wear a suit. The professor wore brown chalk-stripe dress pants and a matching suit vest over a white dress shirt rolled up at the sleeves. The man wrote on the board with practiced grace before stepping away to reveal his handiwork, a sun in the sky circled by squiggly rays of light.

"Sunlight. Some argue it is as elusive a substance as time, but no, it lights this very room, and the playground outside. But it burns like hellfire. Never go into the light, dear boys, at least not without sunblock."

The room fell silent. It already had been, but the silence grew oppressive. Parnell searched the haunted faces of the children. They appeared frightened. How severe was the professor that his own students dared not speak? Parnell was not one to judge, but he took an immediate dislike to the man and could not explain why.

Parnell noticed how the professor's gaze remained focused mostly on him, the outsider, rather than the students. Was the man lecturing to a party of one? Was Parnell considered a student after so many years as an instructor? As a visitor to a foreign land, he was happy to learn new things. Parnell met the instructor's gaze and nodded, an invitation to go on.

The professor pointed to the next word on the board. "Energy. Well, you boys have buckets."

The boys finally chuckled and shifted in their seats. Parnell could not help but smirk along. Humor was a good way to reach and teach children. It pleased Parnell to witness the professor use levity in the classroom.

"Even energy gives off heat which can sustain life. But time does not offer any life-sustaining properties. Time, if anything, impedes life. Stealing bits of it with every moment that passes. There is no other earthly element or concept in existence that replicates the elusive nature of time. If one could harness that power, turn it on its head, well, that individual would be immortal, would they not?"

Parnell listened and held his tongue during the class despite wanting to ask one simple question. What subject was being taught? The discussion leaned toward science, but most church science teachers routinely referenced God. With so many scientific areas of study still relying on theories, it was wise to offer God as a solution to unanswered questions. Parnell did as much on his podcast. Yet, inexplicably, the professor avoided any spiritual references.

The professor stopped speaking while drawing something new on the chalkboard. Parnell used the quiet time to study the classroom further. Something was off about the location. The space was bright compared to the rest of the school, but it also seemed somehow changed from the moment he first entered. He could not place the change, but abandoned the thought when a new student entered the room.

Not any student, but one inappropriately dressed. A boy of maybe thirteen entered wearing nothing other than yellow-stained underwear. The child dripped from head to toe as if fresh from swimming. Despite the startling nature of the child's condition, the teacher and other boys paid no mind. The dripping youth walked to the back of the class and sat at a desk next to Parnell. Class continued without interruption. The boy was deathly pale and appeared in shock.

"Are you okay?" Parnell asked the boy.

As soon as Parnell spoke, the world erupted into a painful sound which forced Parnell to place his hands over his ears. The teacher scraped fingers on the chalkboard, a horrid enough sound any time, but made worse by an inexplicable amplification. It was as if the sound produced by nails digging into slate somehow echoed from the bell tower. All the students suffered the effects as well, except for the wet boy seated next to Parnell. That boy remained stoic and upright during the onslaught.

"I do not tolerate interruptions," the teacher announced authoritatively after removing his nails from the board.

"I apologize, but this boy," Parnell started.

"Student. Same as the others, nothing more."

"Excuse me? He is not well. Freezing and damp, at least. Maybe in shock."

Then the bell rang. And like that, the students raced from the room. The wet child rose from his seat and exited lethargically. The boy clearly needed help, but the instructor seemed not to care. Such inaction angered the priest, who tried to rise but got caught in the too-small seat. In the time he untangled himself, the wet boy was heading out the door. Parnell called out to the teacher.

"I would have words," Parnell said.

Too late. The professor had already packed a satchel and headed for the door, ignoring Parnell's request. Parnell stepped forward.

"Sir, I insist you stay behind class. I have significant concerns over…" The teacher exited the room. "Sir!"

Parnell raced out into the hall. The students were already gone, as was the teacher. Unsure of which way they went (the second floor? Dorms upstairs?), Parnell returned the way he came. The bell ceased ringing by the time Parnell arrived back at the playground.

Sister Camelia sat on one half of a seesaw, her butt on the ground. *More flexible than me*, Parnell thought. Upon spotting him, she rose.

"Unacceptable, all of this. Though I remain unable to understand why I am here, I do have several complaints to make. Please do not distract me with promises of more tours. I insist on seeing the headmaster this instant."

"Sorry, I do not have a time machine," the sister said.

"Excuse me?"

"This building has not had a headmaster in eighty years."

"What? How odd. I suppose based on the condition of the school, they are lacking in funds and therefore could not afford a headmaster. Fine, let me at least talk to the professor who rudely walked away from me."

"No teachers for eighty years, either. Nor students."

"Not true. I just sat in a classroom with them. A roomful of students, and a lecturer obsessed with subjects inappropriate for their age. No headmaster, fine, but who is in charge here?"

"That is the question we ask you to solve, father. That is why you are here. This school closed eighty years ago amidst a scandal involving the death of a student."

"What are you talking about? I saw them,"

"As have others before you. Though not everyone can see them. It requires an open mind, which can be difficult to come by in our field as the church thrives on single-mindedness, where certain concepts are concerned. When they informed me that you were coming, they provided little information other than your openness to certain controversial concepts."

"Paranormal? That is my hobby. My podcast serves as a bridge to explore where religion and the unexplainable intersect. Because God works in mysterious ways, I attempt to resolve some of those mysteries. I have studied enough that I am open to the possibility of spirits trapped on our plane." Then it dawned on Parnell, what the sister implied. "What are you saying?"

"I am not offering an opinion. I await yours."

"Ghosts? Plural. Absurd. What trick are you all playing? Where did the children go so quickly?"

Parnell scoured the courtyard. The forest in the distance could hide an army, but it was simply too far away for that many students to have fled to in such a short time. Parnell examined the surroundings. There was only one answer. The dorms. The students must have never left the building. Camelia appeared to read his mind. She stepped aside.

"I'll be here when you get back," the sister said.

Parnell reentered the building and took the stairs two at a time to the second floor. There, a sea of caution tape greeted him. The corridor was awash in shadows and darkness. Random holes in the ceiling created shafts of light, but they were narrow and distant. Interior windows did little to help, as most of the doors in the corridor remained closed.

The priest threw open the first door and recognized it as the same medical room he had seen through the ceiling from the first floor. He opened the door opposite the hall, which appeared to be a medical recovery room. It was in dreadful disrepair. Overturned beds filled the rooms. Moldy bedding sat in half-dried puddles. Wet patches around cracks in the ceiling showed where the water would have poured in during rainstorms.

Parnell rushed down the hall, exploring every room until it became clear no one was hiding on the premises. Then it hit him. He remembered something about the lower level that might prove the boys were physically present. Parnell rushed down the stairs (almost stumbling headlong after stepping on a piece of rubble). He arrived at the classroom door. The conditions were horrendous, but those conditions would out any mischief because of the dust.

In dust, God had provided the priest with a clue. While noting the school's poor condition, Parnell had earlier noticed the thick layer of dust covering the hallway floor. He rushed over to the classroom from earlier, only for his heart to flutter in astonishment.

A single set of footprints. His own. But students had been there in the class. Parnell attended the lecture, spoke to the professor. Stunned, he entered the classroom and discovered the class to be in the same disrepair as the rest of the school. Earlier, it was pristine. Or was it? Parnell grew confused.

Parnell stumbled back into the corridor. "Impossible."

Whatever tricks they were using to fool him, Parnell could not figure them out. He had to give the children credit. Clearly, hazing was afoot. But there was one thing the boys (and the instructor) had likely forgotten about. Dust on steroids. The courtyard leading to the playground. Because it was mostly dirt, it would capture every footstep of fleeing children.

The priest exited the building, and moved to the playground where he discovered only two sets of footprints. His and hers. Parnell went pale. The nun stood at the courtyard's center, where her shadow melded with an object behind her.

Parnell struggled to comprehend the situation. The only thing that made sense was that Parnell had perished earlier on the mountainside, swooped over the edge along with his luggage. Except as lovely as the grounds were, the school was no heaven. That meant one thing. The class, the boys, the teacher, all of them, they were...

Ghosts.

Parnell stumbled forward in a daze, staring at the building as he walked. He searched the windows and expected to see boys' faces pressed against the glass, laughing, telling him they fooled him. But there was nothing to be seen through the dirty windows. Sister Camelia extended her hand, offering a bottle.

"Water?" Sister Camelia asked.

With shaking hands, Parnell took it and removed the cap. "Yes, water is good."

"And your chair," she said, stepping aside to reveal a single wooden chair she had placed on the dirt playground.

Parnell dropped into the seat. He gulped the water in one go while staring at the building.

"Class is dismissed until tomorrow. Please rest. I am sure you are tired from the drive. I have much to do and will be in the quarters when you are ready to talk," the nun said.

She smiled her good-natured smile before heading back toward the main building. Parnell called out from his chair.

"How do I know you are real?" Parnell asked.

She returned to him. "Please take no advantage of what I am about to suggest. But you are welcome to touch me."

Parnell reached out, tapped her shoulder, then gripped it, needing the anchor. He nodded. "Good. Good," Parnell said.

"And you can let go now."

"Yes. Right."

Though afraid to, Parnell let her go. The good nun headed back to the main building. Parnell watched her go until he was alone in a chair in a schoolyard, one where boys apparently still studied but no longer played.

From where Parnell sat, he could see the top floors of the bell tower behind the dormitory. What appeared a delightful architectural achievement earlier now felt ominous, given the new circumstances. Who rang the bell that morning? Was it the professor? The man looked as if he stepped from silent-movies, handsome but devilish. It was the devilish part that worried Parnell.

Be sober-minded; be watchful. Your adversary, the devil, prowls around like a roaring lion, seeking someone to devour. Parnell remembered the Biblical verse while considering the headmaster. The priest had first attributed his ill feelings about the man to the conditions of the orphanage. Knowing what he did now, Parnell reassessed his gut feelings about the professor.

Too severe, too unwelcoming. That was what came to mind. The church was a sanctuary for those most in need of God's kind hand. Churches were designed to welcome, not deny, pilgrims seeking solace and warmth. Yet the professor had made clear his distaste for visitors. This was a man who had a flock and wished to welcome no more. But why? And where did the man intend to lead his flock?

The priest spoke to the sky. "Dear Father, am I to believe this man is real? Have you brought me here merely to test my faith? I do not understand my place in this, something that seems so sinister."

And sinister it was. Parnell had failed to notice earlier, but all the stone crosses built into the building facades had partially crumbled. Whether worn by time or vandalism, various stone crosses atop building peaks were all desecrated.

Parnell sat for some time, lost in thought and wonder. A class full of boys. As real as he and the nun. They were there and even watched Parnell enter the class. The boys reacted to scraped nails on a chalkboard. They appeared to experience everything as a group.

In times of crisis, there was always one answer. Pray. Parnell bowed his head. He first thanked the Lord for the kindness of the nun, and the comfort of a chair for surely, he could not stand in the aftermath of such a startling revelation. The priest prayed for wisdom and prayed for the souls of the boys. Something struck the priest.

"Ow!" Parnell yelled and looked back as far as he could while seated.

The stone that struck him rested on the ground at the chair's feet. Based on the size, he thanked the Lord that it hit his back and not his head. Parnell rose and turned to face whoever was responsible.

"Who is there?"

The playground was empty. No one was there. Or were they? The push merry-go-round spun in a slow circle. The day was warm and there had been no breeze. Yet the merry-go-round moved as if recently used. But by whom?

"Show yourself."

Another stone sailed through the air. Parnell caught it in his peripheral and attempted to dodge, but the stone struck his shoulder. *Sign that kid up for the Red Sox*, Parnell thought. There were no large rocks anywhere on the playground. Only dead grass, scrub, dirt, and the two rocks that struck him.

They had to come from the outer perimeter of the school grounds. He eyed the forest ahead and noticed a well-worn path. Parnell headed toward the spot. Once past the playground, the grass grew green once again, leading off into a lush forest. Despite the sunlight at his back, the dense forest ahead appeared preternaturally dark.

The utter gloom unnerved the priest, but he attributed his worries to uncertainty over which animals roamed the lands. Back home he knew which states had bears (brown or black), which had mountain lions or bobcats, and even what areas of the country had rattlesnakes. For all he knew, the trees ahead acted as a curtain to all the above.

"Hello."

No stone throwing this time. Thick tree trunks lined both sides of the trail. The branches above crossed over the path and intertwined with one another like fingers clasping. The lush green canopy blocked out most of the sunlight, creating a dark tunnel. A perfect place for a boy to hide.

Despite everything Parnell had seen since arriving, he held out that there was some larger prank ongoing. The boys were **too** real. The rocks that struck him more so. But thrown rocks were a sign of poltergeist activity. Except poltergeist activity limited itself to a single room or home. What were the chances spirits were present on a wide-open mountain landscape? More likely was the possibility that corporeal students were involved in a conspiracy to haze their new instructor.

"I demand you come out here right now. Punishment will be more severe if you do not show yourself immediately," Parnell said, bluffing.

Parnell was counting on the built-in guilt that religious structure instilled in children (lasting into adulthood) to force the perpetrator out into the open. But no rascal appeared. Alive or dead.

Throwing caution to the wind where wildlife was concerned, Parnell decided it was time to walk the path. Or that was the plan until a shadow overtook his own. Parnell's shadow stopped just short of the forest entrance and merged with a much larger one that swallowed his own.

The larger shadow kept growing, and as it did, it took shape, morphing and twisting into something frightening. It seemed to grow hands with dagger-tipped fingers. A head formed, a body stretching into life. (Were those tusk shadows jutting from an oversized head?) Parnell spun to locate the source.

Sister Camelia stood there. "You have been out here longer than I expected. I have dinner ready."

"Dinner? I..." Parnell started before fading off.

Glancing to his feet, Parnell followed the shadow that had swallowed him to the campanile. What first appeared as a twisted version of a beast sneaking up on him was merely the bell tower's shadow caught in the fading sunlight.

"Are you okay, father?" Camelia asked.

"No. I am shaken, as you might imagine. But dinner sounds quite good. Thank you. Where does that path lead?"

The nun spoke over her shoulder as she led him back to the main building. "The well, and places beyond."

"Oh. Should I fetch water to carry back with us?"

She turned back to face him. "No. Sebastian delivers our water supplies. The well is... contaminated."

For the first time since Parnell met the nun, she appeared distraught. Before he could quiz her further, she entered the main building. Parnell turned back toward the path. A shiver overtook him. The night brought with it a chill.

He rushed to catch up to his host, happy to seek shelter in God's house, even one fallen into disrepair and cloaked in mystery.

The nun led the priest back through the church to the connecting corridor, which led to staff living quarters. The corridor was the same where Parnell first saw a boy. (Or had he?) Soon they arrived at a clean, well-stocked kitchen that seemed far removed from the decay of the rest of the orphanage. It even had power, which meant there was a generator.

Parnell's stomach rumbled when a pleasing aroma reached his nose. Multiple pots simmered on the stove. Sister Camelia had been hard at work while Parnell sat on the playground contemplating the impossible. Nothing made sense, and he remained in a daze. Nothing in his podcasting prepared him for a classroom of boys no longer among the living. He did his best to remain focused on the new surroundings.

A door at the rear of the kitchen opened into twin corridors leading to living quarters—hers and his. Sister Camelia handed the priest his black satchel (that he had lost track of) and escorted the man to his room. The space was standard for a priest of Parnell's stature. The room contained a bed, a desk, and a standing wardrobe. Parnell placed his satchel on the desk and opened the wardrobe, which contained clean and pressed priest's garments that appeared his size. Camelia never stepped beyond his doorway; nuns never did lest scandal brew.

"Dinner is ready, but I understand if you need more time to reflect and pray," Camelia said.

"After what I have encountered today, I would prefer to reflect on a full stomach."

Together, they returned to the kitchen. After praying, they dug into a stew loaded with large chunks of meat and vegetables. Parnell almost forgot about the mysteries at hand. He looked at the sister after tasting the soup.

"You could open a restaurant," Parnell said.

"Thank you, but I have an occupation. I did, however, study culinary arts."

"Studied well. Is it a passion of yours? Food and cooking?"

The nun lowered her own spoon and placed her hands in her lap. She gave the question some thought before answering. "I believe God's creatures deserve a bounty that some have delegated only to those rich in cash. Long have I sought equality in the quality of food afforded those rich only in spirit."

Parnell nodded, impressed. "You care about these boys." Parnell stopped, set down his spoon.

"Father?"

"I just spoke about the children as if they were actual students. Despite my faith, despite my tangential interests, I cannot rectify in my mind that the boys do not exist."

"But they do," Camelia said, leaning forward. "Or did. The church has records, knows who most of them were. Father, if I may…"

Camelia looked at the priest with eyes acting as a dam to words ready to spill out. It would take only a bit more water for the levy to break. Parnell nodded.

"There were no sexual inappropriate events at this school." She made the sign of the cross against her chest. "I made certain of that before taking this job. I had no wish to be part of a coverup and sadly, in all faiths, there is some precedent. But it does not mean there was not some form of abuse. Abuse takes many forms. Even if the staff is kind and caring, fellow orphans could be cruel, though most were kind. I would know."

"You were an orphan," Parnell said.

Sister Camelia nodded. "I grew up with a single mother who married a man with children of his own. He decided I was not worth the bother and he, my mother, and stepsisters moved away. I remained in the apartment for a month, fending for myself before neighbors took notice. I ended up in an orphanage. The professors and nuns were kind, and I eventually found my path. Years later, as an adult, I tracked my mother down. My old family had done well, escaped the poverty we grew up in. After sharing with my mother stories of where my life had taken me, do you know what she said?"

Parnell shook his head. "No."

"My mother said, 'The reason no one ever understood you was because they did not live the life you lived.' Such an odd thing to bring up."

"I do not fully understand. Who didn't understand you?" Parnell asked.

"When we initially melded families, there were suddenly aunts, uncles, people I came to care deeply about. I gained a family when my mother remarried even though my stepfather always resented me. The balance of his family brought me comfort and joy. What my mother suggested was that none of them ever understood me. According to her, I was this odd little child that needed to be abandoned because I did not fit in. I was only ten years old when she left me. I did not wish for much in my reunion with her, but her using our time together to suggest those I loved did not love me back, that I was the odd person out made me feel as if I was an orphan all over again. Like I was sleeping in that strange bed that first night all alone. We said our goodbyes without her offering any updates on my sisters or relatives. My mother filled a moral obligation by meeting with me, then bailed for the second time in my life."

Tears danced around the perimeter of the woman's eyes. Parnell longed to reach out, clasp her hand or shoulder, but it was inappropriate from every angle. She smiled, but this time it did not spread to her eyes. Posturing. It was enough to stop the tears, though. She released the smile and stood.

"These boys do exist. Ask anyone in your life if they know an orphan. They might know an adult who once was like myself, but none will ever know orphans at a young age. People look away, like they do the homeless. All God's creatures, all suffering, but no one there to care. No one to acknowledge that they exist, that they too are people with hopes and dreams, who long for the companionship of others. If someone does not stand up for the weak, then what is the church for? Most who come here cannot even see the boys. Others only do after a lengthy stay. You saw them right away. A boy greeted you. I think they are hungry for help. They have danced with the Devil in that classroom long enough. Someone needs to show them another way. I beg of you, father; please don't say they are not real. They need someone. Those lost always need someone."

No need to reach out to her any longer. Though damaged by her past, it had made her strong. The priest had more questions, though, and gestured for her to sit. She refused.

"I will retire for the night. Sleep well."

She exited, leaving Parnell with his stew. He had many questions, but they would wait. He would finish his food and retire as well. It was dark, late, and he was jet-lagged.

He lifted a spoonful of stew to his mouth but spilled it when a piece of silverware struck the floor behind him. Parnell turned.

"Hello?"

A door sat open at the rear of the kitchen, and on the floor sat a fork. Parnell rose, picked up the fork and looked through the door he had failed to notice earlier. Of course, there would be a dining area for guests. The door led to a large dining room filled with banquet style tables and wooden chairs from a bygone era. It was hard to see, but moonlight partially illuminated the room. Another door sat closed at the rear of the dining hall.

Calling out once more but receiving no reply, the priest retrieved the fork and placed it in an open silverware drawer. No telling where it fell from, but he had not even noticed the open drawer earlier. Likely, the sister had left the fork precariously perched. He closed the drawer and returned to his stew.

Ting!

The second time startled him more than the first. Parnell nearly used the Lord's name in vain. The first time was startling, nothing more, but repetition brought with it a sense of foreboding.

"Who is there?" Parnell cried, rising from his chair.

The silverware drawer sat open once again, and a fork rested in the same spot as earlier. Unable to locate the light switch in the dining room, the priest searched the kitchen and found a flashlight. He turned it on.

Stepping over the dropped fork, the priest aimed the flashlight into the dining hall. The beam only traveled so far, so he entered the room, listening for signs of movement.

"Hello?"

Ting!

Silverware hit the floor again. This time at the rear of the dining hall. The priest rushed to the back of the room and startled himself when the flashlight beam reflected toward him from a back door window frame. There, at the foot of the door, sat another fork. And something else.

Wet footprints.

Parnell opened the door and exited. A path led away from the doorway, splitting off in two directions. One led to the side of the dorm that housed the playground, and the other led to the opposite side of the dorm nearest the bell tower. More wet footprints glimmered in the moonlight, leading toward the campanile. Child-sized footprints.

"Show yourself. I mean no harm."

The circular brick tower rose as one large tube until tapering at its peak where it housed the bell. Parnell had glimpsed the top floors when he first arrived at the church. The tower contained no functioning doors or windows, only openings approximating the size of both. At the base of the tower, a high arched doorway (minus the door) sat wide open, permitting entry to all.

Large square openings the size of windows appeared on every floor between the first and the bell. Moonlight showed through some of the openings, revealing twin windows on the opposite side of the tower. No stained glass, no sashes, just cutouts like old castles in England.

The Swiss-cheese style tower rose six stories high. Together, the combined openings would amplify the bell's volume. But architecture was not what he was searching for. He sought movement, which he spotted when a shadow shifted just inside the doorway. The shadow bolted and vanished inside.

"Wait!"

The priest entered the bell tower. A row of stone steps rose from floor to bell tower in a spiral that wrapped around the entire tower's interior perimeter. The first floor was a debris pit filled with souvenirs of collapsed upper floors. A massive hole centered the structure, dropping to unknown depths.

Before the priest could investigate further, he spotted the boy one floor above on the stairs. The child climbed and Parnell chased him. If the stairs ever had a railing, it no longer did. The stone steps were eerily reminiscent of the cliffs leading up to the orphanage: precipitous and ready to accommodate a fall.

Parnell pressed himself against the stone wall as he climbed. Occasionally the boy passed through shafts of moonlight, which allowed Parnell to recognize him as the wet child from the classroom. The boy appeared so pale as to be translucent when the moonlight washed over him.

The climb was taxing and perilous, but Parnell kept on. He ascended three quarters of the tower and caught up to the boy. Or he thought he did. The priest cried out, windmilling his arms as he looked at the ground below. The stairs were missing just below his toes. A gap existed where a section of steps had fallen away, likely into the put below. One more step, twitch, or breath, and he would have fallen to his death.

Several feet away, atop slightly higher ground where the stairs picked up again, stood the boy. The two faced one another across the gap. The boy had to have leaped to reach such heights. Parnell could not fathom such a folly. The boy stood right at the edge of the broken stairs. Parnell reached out.

"I promise I won't hurt you. It's not safe here. Let me help you down. Take my hand."

Parnell reached out to the boy and noticed how the child appeared exactly as he had in the classroom. Soaking wet and wearing only underwear. Seeing the child for the second time allowed Parnell to better guess his age as around twelve or thirteen.

"These stairs aren't safe. I want to talk, but we must get down first. Please," Parnell said, extending his hand further.

Parnell pressed his back against the wall to brace himself for the boy's weight. The boy finally reached out. Parnell nodded to prod the child.

"There you go. I will pull you back to safety. Go on, take my hand."

Their fingers almost touched when the boy fell. (Or leaped?) The boy spread both arms as if crucified, turned, and toppled off the stairs.

"No!" Parnell yelled.

The boy dropped like an angel. A moonlight beam captured the entire fall. The boy looked unceremoniously calm and kept his gaze locked on Parnell. It was only when the boy hit the ground that the shadows swallowed him whole. A loud splash accompanied the child's crash to earth.

Parnell raced down the seps despite the danger of moving so quickly on crumbling infrastructure. There was no surviving a fall from such a height, but Parnell held hope for a miracle. He silently prayed as he ran, begging God to save the boy. The back of Parnell's brain tingled with the knowledge the boy was not alive. Parnell placed faith in a God he could not see and believed that ghosts possibly existed as echoes of lives previously lived, yet the priest struggled to comprehend that the child was not real.

Though the priest could not see where the child landed, he thought he saw a stone well rising from the center of the bell tower. It was hard to lock on the image as it flickered in and out of his bouncing flashlight beam while he ran down the stairs. He had not seen a well when he entered, nor any source of water, but then he was in a chase almost from the start. Parnell had given the ground floor only a cursory glance before partaking in a foot chase on the stairs.

Like water in a desert, the well proved to be a mirage. It vanished as soon as Parnell stepped off the stairs. Only the debris field from earlier remained. Parnell approached cautiously, worried the edges might give way. Aiming the flashlight at the hole revealed it did not drop far, but was filled with rebar, chunks of cement, and a long metal rod bulbed at one end.

The bulbed metal rod appeared to be the bell's clapper. How did the bell ring if there was no clapper? But then, how did boys appear in a classroom lost to time and rot? And how did a boy who was no longer alive fall off the stairs? The only relief granted to Parnell was the absence of a child's twisted body. Small victories. Small miracles.

A wind poured in and struck up a chill, though Parnell was already cold. Blankets sounded good, as well as sleep. The priest returned to his room and slipped into bed. His thoughts threatened to keep him awake for a lifetime, but the travel had done its job. Within minutes, he was asleep in a dreamless slumber.

The church bell woke the priest. Parnell leaped from bed, shocked by how bright the day was already. A knock on the door fell in time with the bell's chime. It had been years since Parnell slept late, which left him in a foggy fugue. Crossing to his standing dresser, he chose from liturgical vestments. Not the entire formal outfit, but a robe. He wished to represent his faith despite not leading a service. Plus, the robe would hide his otherwise sloppy appearance. There was no time for a shower.

Grabbing his satchel, he opened the door. Camelia appeared frantic. She turned and led him away the second he answered the door. She spoke over her shoulder as they walked through the kitchen.

"Do you always sleep so late?"

"No. Only mornings after watching a boy from the top of the bell tower fall into a well that doesn't exist."

The statement caused the nun to lose a step, but only for a moment. If Parnell's honest answer threw her, she did not let it show. She led him through the dining area and to the courtyard outside. Parnell took in the view in the light of day. The same place he was the night before.

"The bell tower is dangerous even during the day. I do not recommend going there again."

"Concern noted."

Aware of the classroom location now, the priest overtook sister Camelia. As he neared the school's entrance, he noticed the nun's absence. She stood yards away. Odd that she only went so far, but there was no time to ask her about it. Parnell entered.

Class was already in session. Everyone remained seated, but there was no sign of the boy from the tower. Parnell took the same seat as before. On his way, he observed the boys observing him as he entered. The professor eyed the man as well and grimaced as if something offended him. (The lateness or the robe?)

"Sorry I'm late," Parnell chanced saying.

Ignoring the late student, the professor pointed to a chalk drawing of a Mobius strip. The Mobius strip was a closed spiral loop with no entry or exit, An infinite loop. The professor wore the same outfit from the day before and looked polished. Where Parnell had battled unease about the man a day earlier, now he only saw the movie star. The professor continued his lecture.

"Does anyone know what a Mobius strip is?" No one raised their hands, so the teacher continued. "Designed by August Ferdinand Mobius in 1858, the Mobius strip is a perfect representation of time."

While looking out at the students, the professor glimpsed Parnell once again and growled once more. He had not acted that way the day prior, so the priest assumed it was related to his religious clothing. Students slunk back in seats, not immune to the teacher's rage. With an angry grunt, the professor returned to the board.

"The Mobius strip serves as the perfect endless loop. It has practical science applications that you all could learn some day if you graduate, but for now we will limit the discussion to time. Imagine you are riding a bike. You fall off the bike and skin your knee. Choose any point on the Mobius strip and say that is where you fell and skinned your knee. If the entire strip represented that one moment, you would remain in a loop where you fell from a bike and scraped a knee forever. But for most of us, the loop is the culmination of our lives, not simply a single moment in time. Is there an end to time or does it all occur at once? Have we already fallen, already scraped a knee, but also falling right now and scraping knees as I speak?"

The professor made interesting points about time and loops, and other things related to it all, but Parnell had stopped listening. He eyed the doorway and then his bag. Pulling a vial of clear liquid from the bag, he rose and approached the door.

Skreee!

Parnell stumbled. Fingernails on the chalkboard once again, intense, overpowering. The children whimpered, covered their ears. Parnell hated to subject the children to such a thing, but he had earlier formed a plan. The fingernails scraped at a volume that defied comprehension and threatened to draw blood from his ears.

The priest continued toward the classroom exit despite the sonic onslaught. Once at the door, the priest opened the vial and poured holy water across the threshold. A horrendous cry sounded at Parnell's rear. A terrible wail that rose above the screech of nails on chalkboard. It was the screech of a wounded animal. (Or a wounded pack? The voice sounded as many rather than as one.)

When the church bell rang, all other sounds ceased. All that remained was the ringing bell. (A bell minus its clapper.) The priest stepped away from the door as the boys rushed past, eager to leave class. Many eyed Parnell with curiosity during the exodus. Parnell attempted to identify their destination, but the sudden presence of another child in the doorway startled him.

The wet boy stood just outside the door even as the other students somehow exited without disturbing the underwear clad child. In a blink, the other boys were shadows, vanishing into darkened corners of the rotted corridor, returning to a place beyond Parnell's understanding. That left only the soaking child and professor.

As before, the professor packed his briefcase, angrily stuffing teaching materials into the overstuffed case. Parnell had questions for both the boy in the corridor and the teacher in the room. Worried they would vanish soon, he assumed he had only enough time to question one of them. He turned to the professor.

"How is it you are all here in this place?"

The professor slammed his briefcase closed and stormed toward the exit only to stop short. The man snarled once again, but this time at water on the floor. It could have come from the bottle or the boy. Parnell gestured to the proverbial line in the sand.

"Holy water. The boys had no problem with it. You?" Parnell asked.

Parnell lived in a city, understood God gave man instinct. There were predators in the cities, those who would harm others, those who found comfort in the arms of demons rather than angels. Parnell, like other city dwellers, did his best to avoid confrontation with strangers that might lead to violence. One had to read people in the city to get by without incident. God did his best to protect his flock, but sometimes the protection came through common sense and situational awareness.

As the professor moved closer, Parnell understood he was no longer safe. It was his city gut talking. Danger was in the air. There was one other way to protect oneself in the cities. Show no fear. The priest stood firm.

"Please. Let these boys go."

The professor smiled while shaking his head. A solid no. Seemingly unable to cross through the doorway, the professor moved to the furthest side of the classroom, where a large hole opened into the next room. That was when everything happened.

A desk nearest Parnell shook, then rumbled in place like an animal stomping its feet before a charge. The desk skidded across the floor, straight at the priest, who leaped away. The desk crashed into a nearby wall. More rumbling vibrated through the floor.

Every chair in the room fluttered in place, the legs vibrating against the floor as if dozens of student's feet stomped simultaneously. One desk near the back of the room hurtled through the air, falling short of the preacher but striking the floor violently. Then another flew, and another. A waterfall of school desks, all hurtling his way. Each row bringing the danger closer. Soon they would not hit the floor with a thud but strike him.

From across the classroom, the professor smiled even as the wounded cry sounded again. It became clear it was not the cry of a domestic animal. Maybe a hyena, but it sounded so foreign that Parnell felt it belonged to an animal that no longer walked the earth.

The classroom flashed between the pristine version of yore and the current one in disrepair. In the present day, there were many holes in the walls in either direction. The professor exited through one such hole. Parnell returned his focus to the desks that were coming too close and landing with increasing force.

Exiting the room, the priest turned in the doorway, hoping the line of the holy water at the threshold would stop the flying furniture. It did not. A desk rocketed through the doorway at a speed designed to remove a head from a body. Parnell froze as the desk shot toward his face.

A child's hand pulled Parnell away. The desk struck with such force that it embedded itself into the wall. Parnell rose and eyed the strange sight, that of half a classroom desk sticking from the wall, as if a child could sit and float.

It could have been a museum display. Place a frame around it and call it a masterpiece, Parnell thought. Except the masterpiece could have decapitated him. The boy in his underwear walked away, only to vanish in the cascade of shadows down the hall.

Parnell reentered the room to gather his bag. The classroom as the students knew it was gone, replaced by a post-apocalyptic style scene. By blocking the doorway with holy water, Parnell had forced the professor to use a hole in the wall that only existed in the present day. There were no such holes during class. Did the boys spot the change? Did they understand?

Maybe the worlds were not that far removed from one another. No matter how it worked, there was more at play than Parnell could fully understand. Moments earlier, all the desks took flight. But now all the desks were exactly as they were. As if they never moved at all. With one exception. The one aimed at his head remained stuck in the corridor wall.

Only a day prior, Parnell had been so intent on finding the students' hiding place that he ignored how the room had changed from a normal classroom to one of decay when he came through a second time. Even if he had subconsciously noted the difference, he was too busy grasping at straws of a new and unwelcome reality. Parnell wondered if the boys noticed the change and if so, were they confused?

As for the professor, he witnessed the change for certain. The man had walked in both worlds without missing a beat. That said something about the man. Other things that spoke volumes about the professor were his lack of religious garments, his avoiding religious topics in class, and the inability to cross a threshold blessed with holy water. Combined, it all gave Parnell a better idea of what he was dealing with. If the priest was correct, then one thing was clear.

The boys needed his help.

Parnell stormed from the dormitory and marched toward the distant forest. Sister Camelia who had been outside waiting caught up to him. She asked why he was in there so long after the bell. Parnell ignored the question and asked his own.

"Exorcists? You've had exorcists here?"

"Yes. Before my time. It was a folly as there is no one to perform an exorcism on," Camelia said.

Parnell sighed. He was grasping at straws and still forgetting the most important thing. The boys were not alive. Despite one being able to pull him to the floor and save him from a flying desk. But the boy in his underwear was no longer living. Parnell needed to remember that if he was to help them. And to help them, Parnell needed answers.

"Where is the well?" Parnell asked.

Before Camelia could answer, the priest spotted a trail of wet footprints. It was a warm and sunny day. Any such prints should have dried immediately, but they did not. They led straight to the path beyond the playground.

The nun observed the priest as he stormed into the woods. She had seen others come and go, many who appeared partially mad by the time they left. The new priest's movements were frantic, but she felt something different in his demeanor. Not madness. (At least not yet.) She sensed righteous anger. In that, she found that which she had almost given up on. Hope.

They reached the path which remained worn and packed down, having been driven over by rescue vehicles decades ago. The landscape never fully recovered. Pressed grass and exposed dirt stretched into the dense forest like a neglected country road leading straight to their destination.

A large circular wellhead made of stone and cement rose several feet above the ground in the distance. A pickup with a small tank on its bed sat nearby with deflated tires. Tufts of grass rose as high as the truck windows.

Someone had capped the well with plywood matching the diameter of the well. Several large rocks rested on the plywood, holding it in place. The miniature wishing well style roof for the well sat nearby in the brush. One two-by-four sized piece of the well roof remained attached to the stone base. The bolts holding it in place were rusty and loose. Three large nails jutted out near the top of the board, a scrape and Tetanus shot waiting to happen.

The well's mouth was sizeable enough for animals or people to fall in were it not covered. Parnell recognized the well head as the same one he glimpsed in the bell tower. (As impossible as that seemed.) But then, a classroom of ghosts and flying desks were things he once considered impossible. He reminded himself that anything was possible in God's world.

"I've seen this in the bell tower," Parnell said.

Sister Camelia looked surprised, but quickly overcame it. "It is Christian's home."

"Christian?"

"The boy in the underwear. The one who is always late for class. It is where he perished. It is where he remains."

"Why didn't they bury him? He's in the well?"

Sister Camelia circled to the other side, gesturing the priest to follow. Six stone crosses rose from the ground, all unmarked. No dates, no names, and clumped too closely together to be actual gravesites. A memorial, more than a cemetery.

"Six? What happened?"

"As you know, the church teaches compassion above all else. Even discipline, when applied properly, can help young congregants live up to their potential. The church would never condone violence, physical, or sexual," Sister Camelia said.

Parnell rose and clapped his hands to clear the dirt. "Yet there is a history that one cannot deny. But I agree, such situations defy the laws of God and have never been a tenant of the church."

"You passed. That statement was a test. A closed mind, unlike a clock, is never correct twice a day. If you denied any such history, I would have spoken no further about what transpired. What would be the point? God may be infallible, but men are not. With that out of the way, I stand by what I told you before about there being no history of sexual abuse at this school."

"But violence?" Parnell stated more than asked.

"In the form of extreme discipline. The school never had issues until the new headmaster arrived. Father Popa. Popa means priest in Romanian, but he was not of the church at the time of his assignment. He was ex-communicated for repeated violations related to female adult congregants. But his background was in education and the orphanage had disciplinary problems. They hired him as headmaster and professor."

"He never mentioned scripture during his classes. I wondered about that. It is a central tenet of education in religious schools." Parnell shook his head, still over-whelmed at having attended lectures by a dead man.

"Students addressed him as Popa, or poppa as they say in the states. My understanding was the professor held as much sway over the staff as he did the boys, but the man was quick to cruelty through words and actions. He was quick to paddle and subjected children to physical punishments like running laps in extreme heat or cold. The seasons are extreme here. It was during such punishments that several boys perished. One at a time over years. Whatever internal inquiries took place after such incidents; the findings were all the same. Death by natural causes."

Parnell clenched his fists. That was why he disliked the professor, even before the attempted beheading via flying desk. There was something disturbing about the man, and this was it. An educator dismissive of the wellbeing of those in his charge.

"One day, after a conflict with Popa, the professor forced Christian to stand in the corner of a classroom in his underwear. Eight hours. No food, no further bathroom breaks. Christian did not make the assigned eight hours without urinating where he stood."

Sister Camelia stopped. A hitch caught her breath. It was a difficult story to tell. Parnell gave her time, staying silent. She continued.

"While the boys played for recess and Popa looked on from the bell tower, Christian, likely weary from standing but wearier from the loss of friends, walked onto the playground still clad only in his underwear. He understood the well served as the only source of water for the school. He walked with purpose. This was Christian's destination," the nun said.

Parnell looked back toward the school. In the shadows in the distance, he thought he saw a parade of heads, all heading toward the well. The sister followed his gaze but saw nothing. Maybe Parnell had not either. Maybe he did not hear the excited murmurs of children coalescing around one of their own. Perhaps he did not hear nuns and other staff cry out in surprise. Maybe it was merely the wind, though he felt no breeze. Camelia continued.

"You can imagine the uproar. Popa, as was his way, watched from the bell tower. His cries for them to stop fell on deaf ears. Like a pied piper, Christian led the other students into the forest. All followed, sensing great importance in the boy's actions. The few nuns out at the time raced to intercede, but the boys walked too quickly. Once the students reached the well, Christian pushed at the well's miniature roof. Perhaps unsure of the boy's mission, the other children helped Christian, pushing until the wooden structure broke away."

Parnell eyed the well's roof sitting in the grass, wondering if it remained in the exact spot where the boys had dumped it. The structure had dried to gray after years of baking in the sun and now rested in the grass like a pile of brittle bones.

"Christian stepped up onto the rock ledge and said, 'No more,' before throwing himself into the well. The well is so deep it is impossible to see the bottom from ground level. The nuns reported hearing a short struggle in the water before all went silent."

"Good Lord." Parnell went ashen. "The boy sat next to me in class. This is beyond my comprehension. Why would the staff leave the child's body down there? And who do the other grave markers belong to?"

"Three other students, athletic sorts, small enough to navigate the well descended by rope held by Popa and other staff. The boys never returned. It would take time to call in outside rescuers. But damage was done. Water became contaminated, and the onsite storage ran low. The event occurred in the heat of summer. The first outsider brought in to retrieve the bodies perished down there. Unlike the boys, the man's body remained attached to an elaborate harness which allowed coworkers to pull him out. The man had somehow drowned in a matter of minutes after descending, despite having access to a breathing apparatus. Some who researched the events believe the man dislodged his breathing device in fright, spitting it out," Camelia said.

"Oak Island," Parnell mumbled.

"Oak Island?"

"It is a legend shared in certain circles. Circles in which I travel."

"As caretaker, the church briefs me with minimal backgrounds on those who will be visiting. Your podcast stood out to me. Strange topic for a priest."

"I started the podcast because of a young student who once approached me asking about dinosaurs. The third grader struggled to reconcile his religious beliefs taught in Sunday school with the existence of dinosaurs. He loved those things so much and wished to become a paleontologist. He felt he had to choose between his faith and his love of Jurassic creatures. I suggested dinosaurs came before man, reminding him God works on his own time. Dinosaurs were a warmup, life not designed in His image."

Parnell froze as he remembered the bestial cry in the classroom. The shriek felt like it was something not of this earth, or at least not any longer. The wounded cry came from something "other." Maybe from something as ancient as dinosaurs. Not willing to share such a frightening thought with sister Camelia, Parnell shook the memory off.

"The child believed so much in dinosaurs that he could not fully embrace his faith. I realized then that some people needed the ability to question their faith in the open while exploring mysteries of life they otherwise could not explain. With the blessing of the church, I became a podcast host covering paranormal events. Oak Island was one such topic. It involves a mysterious island with a potential curse. Six people lost their lives descending into a shaft thought to contain treasure."

"And six here," the sister said.

"You have explained four. Who are the other two headstones for?"

"Trucking enough water for an entire school up the mountain roads proved dangerous and expensive. The church decided to abandon the orphanage. Drilling a new well was beyond the school's limited finances. When announcing the closure, the church made it clear they were done with Popa as well."

"Finally," Parnell said, exasperated.

"Sadly, the educator was not finished endangering children. Rousing three of the strongest boys from their beds one late night, Popa led them to the well. The professor was intent on retrieving the bodies and rescuing the school. If human remains were removed from the source, the water would eventually run clean once again."

"What happened?"

"Popa instructed the boys to lower him into the well. He hoped to succeed where others had failed. The stories have surely evolved with retellings, but according to records, Popa cried out almost immediately after reaching the water. He yelled for them to pull him up. The frightened boys did as they were told, but as the man neared the top of the well, he looked down the shaft, screaming at something beyond the boys' collective vision. The professor struggled with his grip and, as he crested the lip of the stone wall, he grabbed one child by his nightshirt. But the child could not hold the weight of the man and fell in alongside Popa. The splash of water swallowed their collective screams. Neither one ever surfaced."

"Which accounts for the last two grave markers," Parnell said.

Sister Camelia nodded. "They closed the school immediately. Years later, the church hired workers to salvage what they could from the campus. Those workers were shocked to hear the bell chime. Unable to identify who rang it, they searched the grounds. They discovered a class in session. Or one worker did. The others failed to see anything and declared their coworker mad for fleeing in fright."

"And the class remains in session still."

"Yes. Priests came and went over the years, each performing various religious ceremonies, but nothing changed. Eventually, they assigned a caretaker to oversee the property. I am the latest caretaker and have been here for years. It is a lonely job, but the mountain brings me closer to God, and His grace has given me the opportunity to try to help the poor boys in the classroom, Though I am sad to say I failed. Popa grew increasingly violent until I no longer dared attend class. It took time before the boys even acknowledged me. I believe they are hungry for a father figure, but they know none beyond Popa."

"I understand the violence. I experienced it today." Parnell headed back toward the school, the nun at his side.

"Many never saw the boys. You saw one immediately upon arrival. Further, Popa turned violent within one day of your arrival. He never even bothered with me until the boys acknowledged my presence with stares and turned heads. There is a pattern, a cycle to the strange happenings here, but it has never escalated so quickly before," she said.

"Why do you think that is?"

"Others treated the situation. Exorcise the whole thing away, declare it all evil. But you have not declared it a situation. You are concerned with how best to help these boys. You were concerned about the conditions of the school, not for vanity's sake, but because it was improper for students to learn in such conditions."

"But I did not know there were no students when I first encountered the crumbling buildings," Parnell said.

"Exactly my point. You thought this was a working school, and you were ready to scold Popa, or whoever was in charge. You are correct in one thing." Sister Camelia pointed at the crumbling dorm looming above them. "The boys deserve better than this. They just need someone to convince them of that."

"But how?"

"God sent you here for a reason. You need to decide how."

Camelia walked away, back to the living quarters, leaving Parnell alone in a world he did not understand.

P arnell sat on the seesaw and fell to the ground on the board in a controlled drop. His legs immediately threatened to cramp, and he wondered how the nun had sat there so easily. He hoped a connection to the playground would help place him in the mindset of the students. What were they experiencing? What did they know of their situation?

Parnell studied the dormitory's exterior which had the makings of a haunted place. A world stopped in time, closed and forgotten, a perfect place for a restless spirit to roam. Singular. A collective haunting unnerved the priest more than he let on in front of the nun.

Faith in God did not immunize one from fear. Believing that life's end led people to the promised land still included the process of shaking off one's mortal coil. That experience was known to be painful and often brutal. Five boys suffered such a fate.

To drown, splashing in vain to gain a foothold while fighting for oxygen, would be a horrific way to perish. Parnell found some comfort that in the end, all found peace. Or did they? Somehow, that peace appeared to elude a classroom full of students. Given the number of students, it meant there were other victims as well Ones who succumbed to heatstroke, hypothermia, and heart failure.

Eight windows ran across the top floor and bottom of the dorms. The priest looked away for a moment, but gasped when he looked back. A boy looked out from each window. Parnell cried out in fright and let go of the see-saw handle, which caused him to tumble back onto the ground.

The priest scrambled to his feet and looked up again, but the windows were empty. No one was there, if they ever were at all. Sister Camelia said things recently accelerated. That the boys sought guidance, a father figure. Parnell charged toward the building.

After entering the classroom, the priest freed every desk from the rubble, righting them all. He sought to return some integrity to the room. Holes in the ceiling and walls were beyond his ability to fix, but he needed them. They allowed enough sunlight in for him to work. And the other holes, those opening into equally destroyed classes on either side, gave him a place to dump debris.

After straightening some of the room, Parnell approached the professor's desk and found it to be the darkest spot in the room, hidden in shadows by lack of sunlight or something more sinister. A chill overtook him as he neared the chalkboard. Shaking it off, he returned to the task at hand, dumping chunks of concrete and other debris one at a time into the adjacent rooms.

The work was arduous, the stones heavy, testing his physical limits, but Parnell thought of others in the seminary, friends who volunteered around the globe to do just such work. Parnell helped the church and school in other ways, but now it was his turn for the heavy lifting.

Eventually, Sister Camelia joined him, bringing a picnic basket of fresh fruit, sandwiches, and, most importantly, two snow shovels. She explained the winters were heavy with snow and plows were not readily available on the mountain. Sadly, two boys in the class perished while shoveling as punishment. Such was the nature of the abuse.

The nun and priest worked in tandem, chatting while they cleaned the room. The sister shared more of what she knew of the orphanage's history. Which victims perished when, and in what manner. Despite the professor being responsible for many of the deaths, as headmaster he was also in charge of the investigations. At least until the church noticed a pattern and took over. (The church quickly shut the place down once they learned the truth, but not until after Christian's fall.) Popa's investigations omitted the names of the victims. It was as if he wished to leave the victims in limbo, vanish their existence from the world. Or at least the physical world.

The priest and nun sweated in the physical world, working hard to make the space look like a classroom again. In an act of defiance, Parnell freed the desk from the corridor wall and returned it to the back of the class, though the hole remained as a reminder of Popa's wrath.

The couple worked until the sun went down. By the time they were done, the room had filled with shadows that flickered with movement. Some seemed to follow them around the room, but whenever they examined the darkened corners, they came up empty.

Sister Camelia announced she would return to the kitchen to warm up leftovers for dinner. Parnell said he would join her soon. He had one thing left to do.

The priest scoured the chalkboard and the floor around it for a piece of chalk but found none. A search of the professor's desk failed to produce any. Something shifted in a nearby debris pile on the other side of the hole that Popa had exited through.

"Hello?" The priest called out. No answer, of course. Parnell peered through the hole. While unable to find what made the noise, he noticed the chalkboard next door and decided to give that one a go. Rather than exit through the door and reenter the other room, Parnell followed Popa's footsteps and stepped through the hole.

He gasped in horror as the world changed. Images of a fiery landscape flashed through his mind. In those images, four-legged animals walked on two and punished humans trapped in walls made of brimstone. Chambers and passages fed off in all directions, a labyrinth of victims trapped in the foul-smelling stone. The cavernous walls fed off in infinite directions.

People's body parts jutted out from the brimstone walls, a head here, an arm there, breasts, penises, legs, occasionally buttocks and backs of a torso. It was like a sea of mannequin parts arranged for a nightmare art exhibition, except all the body parts moved. The faces, where visible, cried out in agony and tortured ecstasy. The heat was unbearable.

As fast as the image flashed to life, it vanished. Parnell stumbled the rest of the way through the hole into the next room. He fought to regain control of his senses. It was as if walking in Popa's footsteps revealed another world, one in which the professor ruled with others of his kind.

Like a dream, the memories of what he glimpsed quickly vanished in a brain fog. Were those animals harming men and women? Were they even animals? Did a child's innate innocence spare them from existing in such a world? For Parnell mercifully saw no trapped children, only adults of every nationality. The labyrinth went on forever, of that, he was sure. An endless universe of misery and hopelessness.

Soon the priest could not lock onto any of the images he glimpsed. The memories faded even as he remembered his purpose for entering the other classroom. A rat scurried away, likely responsible for the rubble shifting that drew him to the hole. (Had a massive rat walked on two legs in that other world?) Parnell shook off the vague recollection and searched the new classroom for chalk but found none.

Something sounded in the hallway. He spun around and saw a shadow run past the open doorway. Parnell raced out into the hall and found a single set of wet footprints. Alongside the footprints that faded before him, sat the very thing he sought. A single piece of chalk.

The priest picked it up, returned to the classroom and wrote on the board.

The next morning, Parnell rose early and prayed. He prayed for answers, for the safety of the boys, and for wisdom to defeat what the priest believed to be demonic forces at play. Most of all, Parnell prayed he was not going mad. When he sat with the boys, they were real to him.

And as such, they were students to protect and educate. But at night, while he struggled to sleep, doubt seeped into his mind. Mass hallucinations were not unheard of. Perhaps there were spores or mushrooms of mysterious origin growing somewhere on the abandoned property.

Madness, artificial or otherwise, made sense when considering the alternative. An abundance of spirits gathered in one place made little sense. Ghosts were solitary, lonely things, trapped in the chains of a tragic or unsatisfying end.

Worse, the images Parnell experienced when he followed Popa's footsteps (that he could barely remember and wished to forget) only added evidence to the possibility that madness had overtaken his senses.

Insanity was perhaps the best alternative, for if the boys were not a figment of Parnell's splintered mind, it meant Hell truly existed. Heaven's existence required a leap of faith for many, including true believers. The priest felt trapped in a world where belief in Heaven required faith, but Hell existed as a point of fact.

A knock interrupted Parnell's praying. Through the door, sister Camelia urged the priest to join her for breakfast, but he declined, needing fuel for his soul, not his body. He prayed until the bell rang. A part of him hoped the bell would not ring that day, that the line of holy water would stop the mad professor from even returning to class.

No such luck. The priest rose to his feet and exited the room.

Sister Camelia accompanied Parnell to the dormitory. Once there, Parnell asked the sister if she wished to accompany him. She eyed the entrance with longing but shook her head. Parnell never asked what transpired between her and Popa. It must have been horrific. She made it clear that violence was involved, but now he wondered if the nun walked in Popa's footsteps and experienced visions of her own.

As the priest headed back to the classroom, he wondered why the church had sent him in blind, with no details about the school. Sister Camelia mentioned that many people simply could not see the boys. Perhaps arriving with no preconceived notions was a test. If the visitor failed to experience the class in session, they were sent home packing. (Minus their mountainside luggage.)

A test made sense, but one question weighed heavily on the priest. Why him? The church had unlimited resources and somehow failed to clear the spirits away from the site. Vanity was not one of Parnell's sins. He was nothing special, a mook with a microphone. What could one man and one woman do together?

Fight?

A fighter inside and outside the ring as a youth, Parnell often feared he enjoyed violence more than he enjoyed the sport. Over time, he used prayer to tame his base instincts and walked away from confrontations. He preferred to teach congregants to solve issues with their hearts and heads over fists. If the church demanded a fighter, they chose one who was rusty. Besides, Parnell did not see Popa stepping into a ring anytime soon. Sinners rarely fought fairly.

Class was already in session by the time the priest arrived. The classroom was once again pristine, cleaner even than he and sister Camelia had managed. The words Parnell wrote on the board were absent. He wondered if the boys were able to read the message before they took their seats. Did the world transform with their entrance or was it always locked into another time when they were present? The professor ignored Parnell's arrival. Or so the priest thought.

The boys watched Parnell move to the back of the class, their eyes almost pleading for help or something else. (To be careful?) There was something different in the way they watched him, as if they were waiting for something.

It suddenly became clear when Parnell neared his seat. The desk skidded away from him. Only a few feet, but message sent—*you are not welcome, man of the cloth.* The children turned, either startled by the noise of a desk sliding or waiting for something more.

Parnell refused to be cowed by the professor with his alarming parlor tricks. Rather than take another seat, Parnell reached for the shifted desk with the intent to return it to its rightful position. But the moment he grabbed it, his body went rigid as if electrocuted. Like holding electric cables, he could not let go of the connection. The vision from before struck him with such force it dropped him to his knees.

By the time he hit the ground, the priest was no longer in the classroom but in a labyrinth that spun off in so many directions it made him dizzy. Or perhaps it was the heat that made him dizzy. Having fallen on his hands and knees (no desk in sight) his hands sizzled where they touched the ground. He lifted them immediately, but they still burned in the open air. The priest broke out into a sweat so intense it soaked his clothing, which then steamed under the heat.

The heat threatened to choke the life out of him. His throat went dry, and skin peeled away from his lips. Skin all over his body crackled and cooked. Cries of pain, despair and loss sounded in every direction, but it took him a moment to realize his screams were among them.

Air crackled with the sound of roasting flesh. Liquids, where there were any left sizzled and boiled. Such intense heat was enough to kill him, yet he remained alive. Perhaps death was not an option in such a place, he thought. For what was death but release?

Earth was not eternal, merely a rest stop for the living. Some visited longer than others, but in the end, everyone found peace. A morbid thought perhaps, but as Parnell considered the alternative, it struck him how heavenly a concept it was that everyone eventually found their own peace on earth.

There was no peace in the labyrinth of pain he found himself in. The air shimmered like asphalt in a desert, warping and distorting the already twisted scenery. Unlike stories of such a place, there were no visible flames, only striations of red lining the endless walls of brimstone. (And he only knew it was brimstone from his earlier vision, though how he knew such a thing he could not explain.) Sulfuric gas puffed out from walls, casting a dense odoriferous fog across the hellish labyrinth.

Endless corridors stretched in infinite directions as if to eternity. Rather than being trapped in chains of lore, bodies were embedded in brimstone. Some positioned upright, some upside-down, others trapped in the most twisted positions that surely tested a body's limits.

Body parts were not restricted to only cavern walls, but they also dangled from cavern ceilings and rose the floors. Body parts of every type took up space in the endless tentacles of caves. Not merely heads, but arms, legs, hands, feet, buttocks, and genitalia both male and female. Some showed through the rock walls as singular body parts, while others were parts of a larger whole.

Some exposed heads dangled from the ceiling directly above waist-up legs rising from the cavern floor below. Bodies split for eternity, with those heads positioned to view their own defilement at the hands of horrific beasts that roamed the land.

Collectively, the exposed heads and faces, (for some were tips of a nose and only a mouth showing through the rock) cried out in agony, screamed in tortured pleasure, and wailed in regret. The only relief Parnell found in the endless landscape was an absence of children. He had not seen them before and did not see them now. It suggested true innocence was spared from such an evil place.

But the boys back in the orphanage were trapped in their own way. Maybe not in brimstone, but stuck in place, in time, forever held hostage to the professor's whims. Locked in their own Mobius strip. What hold did the professor have over the students? Was the hellscape used as a lure? Did Popa offer them a way to escape class forever, even if it meant eternal torment? Were the boys to be Popa's prize? The first children to be entombed in eternal misery?

Hooves clopped somewhere in the distance reminding the priest of his initial vision, that of animals walking on two legs. As Parnell watched evil torturers roam the hollowed caverns while punishing those trapped in brimstone, he realized that image was only partially correct. Some did have attributes of animals, but most did not. The abhorrent proprietors of the heated hellscape were varied in their appearances.

One being nearby wore hundreds of eyes across his nude body. The man was fleshy, large, and all his eyes blinked. Eyeballs lined his arms, legs, even his penis. The horrid being approached a trapped woman and dug his fingers into her sockets, removing the orbs one at a time. The woman who had already been screaming upped the volume as the beast tore her eyeballs away.

The eyeball collector pressed one eye into an open spot on his arm, then reached over his shoulder and placed the other on his upper back. The woman's head shot right, then left, looking all around. It was clear she could still see, but through the beast, and from different angles, that would likely drive her to eventual madness.

Many of the torturers were merely men and women starved into thin bodies. All were nude but many wore horrific metal masks that glowed red under the heat. Many of the masked demons sported horns of varying lengths. Some also wore razor wire wrapped over parts of their bodies. Demonic penises and breasts were oversized and distorted.

One 'woman's' breasts twisted in tight corkscrews to sharp points. She stood over six feet tall and wore a necklace of razor wire covered in blood with chunks of human flesh hooked on the individual blades that comprised the necklace.

Both the torturers and those trapped took part in hedonistic activities. Demons slit open holes in trapped bodies before using those holes to defile the bodies. As if the situation was not bad enough for those eternally tortured, some of their own defiled their neighbors. Some trapped individuals that had arms exposed through the stone groped other nearby trapped individuals. Some visible faces cried out in ecstasy, but most simply whimpered, cried, and screamed.

Parnell fought the urge to vomit. There was nothing erotic or enticing about the end of the world. He turned away from an intensely vile act occurring nearby, only to face more of the twisted world. It was endless, this kingdom of pain and despair.

The already unbearable heat grew more so once his sweat evaporated. There was no more moisture to be found in the priest's body. The ground beneath his knees became unbearably hot. Parnell rose from the molten floor, which finally caused those trapped in the walls to notice him. They reacted wildly upon spotting a visitor. They cried out, some begging for help, others demanding sexual favors, and many simply threatening to wear his flesh.

Somehow, in the sea of cries, a familiar voice reached his ears. Stuck in a wall, as if seated in a sling, was Sister Camelia. Her face stuck out of the wall from ears forward. Her arms were outstretched, as were her legs and breasts. The rest of her body remained hidden behind the wall.

The sister grinned at Parnell and batted her eyes. After licking lips, she bit her bottom one. The bite started as sexual hunger before becoming the real thing. The nun bit off her lower lip and chewed on it.

Such a blasphemous image sickened the priest. He worried it was more than a vision. What if it was a premonition? If they failed, would the sister somehow suffer for all eternity? She was innocent, had no right to experience such a place, but what was the nature of Popa's power? Could he influence others to join him, like he did the boys?

No. Parnell refused to succumb to such fears. The priest was not only in a land of debauchery and pain, but he was also in the land of lies. Parnell blinked, and the woman was Camelia no more, never was. He blinked again and found himself back in the classroom, on his knees, soaked in sweat. He let go of the desk, the source of his hallucinations.

The teacher stood alongside Parnell, except it was not Popa, the 1940s movie star. It was a version that belonged to the place Parnell just experienced. Popa wore nothing but tattered pants, covered in singed holes. His exposed torso was all sinew and muscle. Ram horns rose high above his head, surrounded by tufts of black hair that looked like fur. But the worst was reserved for Popa's face.

A combination of metal and flesh came together to create a horrific visage. The man's eyes were metal and slotted like miniature colanders popped over the eye sockets. His nose was a metal pig snout the size of a tin can. The mask split off at the jawline, leaving his mouth exposed. His gritted teeth locked into an evil smile and sharp tusks jutted from each side of his jaw.

Attempting to maintain his sanity, Parnell looked away from the aberration and noticed that all the boys had gathered around him. Parnell's stomach churned. He needed to vomit, but he fought the urge, not willing to show weakness in front of the boys.

"Is there a problem?" Popa said, never using his own mouth. Instead, he spoke through all the boys' voices simultaneously. Proof he controlled the class.

The afterlife chorus sent a shiver down Parnell's spine. Death had its own world, and apparently it was multi-faceted. The horrors not only existed in catacombs of brimstone but in classes locked in time as well. The professor continued to speak through the collective mouths of the students.

"Do you see, class? Only I can prepare you for what comes next. Look how weak this man is. This ambassador of a false deity. He would lead you nowhere. Only I can prepare you for the land of the dark, the land where desires come true," Popa said, using the voice of the boys.

"Liar," Parnell whispered, his voice a croak, dehydrated from heat beyond anything on earth.

Water trickled down Parnell's face, cooling him, bringing him relief where his own sweat failed. The water eased his pain. Parnell spotted the bare feet before he spotted the boy. The crowd had parted to let Christian through.

"No more," the boys collectively said before returning to their seats.

Popa growled again in a chorus of extinct animal cries. Christian extended a hand, reaching for the priest. Parnell looked up at the boy and reached out for help but over Christian's shoulder, Popa smile knowingly. The church bell rang. Popa knew the schedule or controlled the ring at any time. Either way, the boys cleared the room.

Before helping the priest up, Christian reacted to the bell and left as well. Parnell slumped back on the floor. From where Parnell sat, he could not see Popa exit, but he heard the man leave. The footsteps clopped like hooves.

With class dismissed, the room returned to normal. Though still on the ground, Parnell looked to the board and saw his own message: '*God loves you. There is another way.*'

Parnell squinted. Another message covered the lower corner of the chalkboard. Unable to read it from so far away, Parnell rose, stumbling as he struggled to regain his balance with the earth. The message read: '*No more.*'

Cellphones were useless in the mountains, but the alarm function still worked. Rising early was essential to Parnell's plan. He rose when the sun's first rays fluttered above the treetops. The nun who never seemed to sleep was already up and attending to matters in the living quarters. Seeing the priest so early surprised her. More surprising was Parnell's request. Paper towels. She handed him a nearby roll. Parnell took a few sheets and exited through the rear door. Camelia followed. They headed toward the bell tower.

"It is the boy from the well. They listen to him. He is the only reason they have not followed Popa," Parnell said.

"Followed Popa where?" Camelia asked.

The priest stopped short and faced the nun. For the first time since he met her, sister Camelia averted her eyes. Parnell finally understood why the nun no longer dared enter the school. Beyond any physical attacks that might have occurred, a mere glimpse of the land of despair would test anyone's faith.

"I think you know," Parnell said.

The nun turned away. With nothing left to say, they rushed into the bell tower. Parnell stepped down to where the floor had caved in and navigated over rocks as if crossing a brook by stone. Near the tower's center, Parnell gripped the bell's metal clapper, which jutted from piles of concrete. He yanked and stumbled back as his hands slipped off when the bar failed to give. Repositioning himself, he pulled again, but the metal did not budge. Camelia jumped down, moving as effortlessly in her habit as if wearing gym clothes.

She gripped the bell's clapper as well. Their combined efforts caused a slight movement in the device, but large chunks of concrete still held it tight. They shook it back and forth to create a gap, which provided more give. With renewed vigor, they collectively pulled and collectively fell on their asses, but they had the clapper.

From where they sat, the bell above seemed forever away. The building was structurally unsound and grew more so the higher one climbed. Each level looked ready to join the pile below. They rose to their feet.

"You have yet to ask me, but I am certain you wonder where others before you failed. Many left the moment they saw the boys, calling it the Devil's work. Others left after experiencing violence at the hands of Popa. But the most recent visitor took to attending class every day with no results and no suggestions on how to proceed. At dinner one night, the man smiled at me throughout in a manner all too familiar," Camelia said.

Parnell tossed the clapper over his shoulder to relieve some of the weight. "A priest looked at you that way?"

"Not a priest. A hired hand. Someone outside the church who promised results. A paranormal investigator," she said.

"The investigator said he considered taking me but no longer felt the need because the opportunity presented itself every day in class."

Parnell stopped on the stairs and turned back. "Did he mean…"

Before he could finish the question, she answered. "That was exactly what the man meant. It is also the reason I now have a padlock on my door. Not that you would know, because you never bothered to locate my sleeping quarters. Grateful for that, by the way. The investigator never said explicitly, but I believe he travelled to the other place while there. One day he failed to return."

They moved to the stairs. For a moment Parnell thought he glimpsed a well back where they just retrieved the metal rod. It was shadows, nothing more. But he thought of the boy falling from high up on the stairs. They continued talking while climbing the perilous stairs.

"Did the investigator ever mention Christian?"

"Yes, but not kindly. The investigator believed Christian was the problem. He said the drowned boy was the only thing holding the boys back from a destiny of depravity. After such a statement, I knew I was no longer safe in the man's presence, but he vanished soon after. My best chance to find the missing man was to attend a class. Once there, Popa dislocated my shoulder with merely a thought. Furniture flew, and I was down. Worse, he threatened the boys for trying to help me. It was then I suffered a lengthier horrid vision than the first time I experienced one."

"Let us be clear. It is no vision. Popa has the keys to Hell's gates. Of that I am certain."

"What I saw was the missing investigator, naked, transformed into a partial beast. He drooled while conveying his intentions to me. His spittle sizzled on the floor. He reached for me and then, mercifully, I found myself back in class."

Parnell, who had the lead on the stairs, stopped and looked back at her. "That is Popa's weakness."

"What is?" Camelia asked.

"In the sea of faces, there were none I recognized from home. Nor did I see any children. Either of those scenarios would have tortured me to the point of madness. That means Popa is not the Devil. At most, he is a demon, a foot soldier. Well, guess what? We're foot soldiers too."

With that, he climbed, moving as quickly as the dangerous conditions allowed. Soon they arrived at the break in the stairs where Christian had fallen. The gap appeared insurmountable.

"I never climbed these stairs before. No reason to. This seems like a very bad idea," Camelia said.

"Leap of faith, right?" Parnell said, trying to lighten the mood, but sweat popped along his brow and his throat went dry.

He turned and handed the clapper to Camelia. The portion of the clapper that broke off was only about four feet long. The ball at the end was heavy, but manageable. Camelia pressed herself against the wall as the priest descended a few steps, ran, and jumped!

The steep angle made the leap difficult, but the priest made it, though he landed roughly. Camelia yelped in victory. Parnell rose quickly, determined to press on. He stepped toward the stair's edge, reaching for the bell clapper, when suddenly the concrete at his feet gave way. The priest dropped instantly.

And stopped almost as quickly. The crumbled concrete fell to the distant ground, but it left a metal stair pan for a step that was much smaller than the priest's body. The tight opening captured Parnell's legs, keeping him from copying Christian's plummet.

The metal edges of the stair frame dug into his legs, but he was alive. Adrenaline muted the pain. He twisted toward the intact stairs behind him and pulled himself free before climbing to higher ground where the stairs still held.

"Throw it," Parnell said.

Camelia swung the clapper from the lighter end, using the ball's weight to give it momentum. She launched it across the gap. Parnell caught it awkwardly, almost dropping it. The ball's weight threatened to drag it down into the abyss, but it finally settled in the priest's arms. Parnell climbed the rest of the stairs to the bell.

Pulling the paper towels from his pocket, Parnell wadded them and stuck them in his ears. Raising the bar, he swung the ball at the bell. The impact shot pain down his forearms, but it worked. The bell rang, but at a diminished volume compared to the daily classroom call. Fearing it was not loud enough, he chose another spot on the bell and swung harder.

Not the same as an internal ring, it was the best he could do. Parnell hoped the boys would hear it. He struck it several more times before dropping the clapper and returning to the stairs. He descended quickly and yelled for Camelia to clear the way.

She circled down and around until she could see him from the lower floor. There, she would act as a witness to success or failure. Parnell ran down the stairs, leaped and landed on the lower level. From there, he wasted no time. He quickly caught up to the nun, and they rushed out of the bell tower and to the classroom.

Camelia ignored any past fears and followed Parnell into the classroom. The room was not the pristine version of the past, but the one that they had cleaned to the best of their abilities. The ringing bell had done its job, for all the students sat at their desks. Only Christian and Popa were missing. Camelia placed her hands to her mouth and gasped. She took in the faces she had not seen in so long.

Parnell took a deep breath, overwhelmed at the sight of the boys in **his** classroom. He offered them a warm smile. "Hello boys. So good to see you. I believe you all know Sister Camelia."

The boys nodded. Several blushed as Camelia waved to them. They waved back.

"You are probably wondering why I am here. I was a student a long time ago in a classroom very much like this one. You know what I enjoyed the most? Substitute teachers. They were always a pleasant change over the day to day. Don't things get boring when you experience the same thing over and over?" Parnell asked.

The boys eyed one another nervously. Soon their gazes settled on the opening in the wall nearby. Parnell pulled a bottle from his pocket and handed it to Camelia. She walked over to the opening in the wall and poured a line of holy water.

"Do not worry. He is not here. Substitute teacher, remember? I ask again. Raise your hands if everything gets boring when you hear the same thing over and over."

All hands went up. That was his signal, his way of communicating. They were too scared to speak, too afraid of their Poppa.

"Yeah, been there. Let's talk about time. I know you have heard certain things, but do you ever wonder why those lectures are not in your schoolbooks? Or why you do not even have schoolbooks? It is because you are being told, not taught. Raise your hand if you dislike people telling you what to do." Most hands went up. Not perfect, but a start. "Today is a tutoring twofer. Today, you will hear from one of the smartest, kindest people I know. Sister Camelia, can you tell these boys what you told me at the dinner table?"

Camelia stepped away from the hole in the wall and took the floor. "Children. I am so happy to see you. I do not have notes, nothing prepared, but understand I have worked in many places like this. One day, a woman walked into our orphanage and wished to surrender her child. The woman appeared as if she had been in a car accident, so serious were her physical injuries. She held a child in her arms. Toby was his name. When it came time to hand Toby over, the woman refused to let go, could not, but eventually she did."

The nun steadied herself, trying to remain stoic for the boys. Parnell took note of how closely the boys seemed to listen. Camelia continued.

"After she handed the boy over, she collapsed. We brought her to our medical facilities on site and discovered both her arms were broken, yet she had carried that child. There was confusion in the aftermath. It was difficult to tell if she had suffered injuries from an accident or from someone who claimed they loved her. Either way, her last thoughts were how she could best protect her child. Despite our best efforts, the woman did not survive."

Camelia paused, wiped at the corners of her eyes. Then she scanned the faces in the classroom. A sea full of Toby's.

"I understand you might feel abandoned, or like no one cares. But you were all delivered here with love. You are orphans in name only. Somewhere there is a parent who made the toughest decision of their lives. Please know the one who delivered you loved you and those who received you love you as well. If ever you feel despair and loneliness as vast as the universe, just know your heart will find its home if you open it up," Camelia said.

Parnell wrote '*You are loved*' on the chalkboard. "Thank you, Sister Camelia. How do I follow that? By quoting one of your friends. Someone you all know. No more! When have you had a summer break? When have you had recess? Who misses playing on the playground?" All hands went up. "The church may have me fired for this, but I think it is well past the time you all skip class." Laughter erupted in the room. Parnell laughed along. "Imagine that. A teacher telling you to skip class. There are alternatives, boys. I need you all to follow the light. This classroom is no place for boys like you."

Darkness descended over the classroom, prompting a collective murmur of concern from the students. Like an old TV seeking a signal, the classroom flashed back and forth between the past and the present. The priest and nun eyed one another, understanding. The heavy breathing of hyenas and exotic beasts sounded from all directions while clopping hooves drew closer.

Popa appeared outside the hole in the wall. He cried in the now familiar chalkboard screech but remained outside, unable to step past the line of holy water. Camelia covered her ears, trying to block out not only the moment, but memories from a past encounter. The floor shook, and all the loose desks trembled in place, as if they too were afraid of the man who sought entry.

"I will punish you all for this, children. Have I not taken care of you? Have I not shown you the way?"

"You fed them lies. Follow the light boys. Do not cower in the darkness any longer. Seek the stars where only darkness prevails. Find your way home!" Parnell yelled before the world exploded.

Vibrations in the desks sent the boys scrambling to their feet. The empty desks spun in circles before shooting toward the ceiling. Papers on Popa's desks fluttered into a cyclone, the white pages turning red, each page bleeding out. An apple on the desk melted into rot with maggots gnawing on the decayed flesh.

The students huddled together in the room's center, riding out the wrath of their professor. Parnell continued yelling to the boys, but the chaos in the room drowned out the priest's voice. Hurricane style winds threatened to tear the place down.

Camelia saw it first and cried out. Too late. The teacher's desk rose and flew at Parnell. Camelia pushed the priest out of the way, but the desk struck her and carried her across the room, pinning her to the wall. The priest rushed over to help the trapped nun.

"No more!" Christian yelled from the doorway. He waved to the other students, who quickly rushed to follow the boy.

"Stop! Where are you going? There will be consequences for all!" Popa cried.

The boys dodged falling desks as, one by one, the furniture dropped back down from the ceiling. Christian ushered his classmates through the door.

Parnell pulled the desk away from Camelia who fell onto her side, assessing the damage. She was still conscious but in pain. Parnell reached out to help, but she waved him off.

"Go. Do not lose the boys. Go!" Camelia yelled.

Except Parnell had lost them. The corridor was empty. He rushed to a room across the hall and looked out the window. From on high, he spotted the boys following Christian into the forest. Parnell gave chase. Despite being far behind, he had a trail to follow. Wet footprints led the way. The footprints were always a sign.

He arrived at the well but saw no sign of the boys. He dislodged the well cover and peered down, battling vertigo. The well mouth was wider than permits allowed back in the US. He could not see the bottom it ran so deep. The well's interior appeared to be a void, a place where light went to die.

The well contained five boys already. Had the others descended with Christian? Were they safer there? Had the drowned child led the others to a safer place? Parnell placed his hands on the stone wall and leaned further. Parnell remembered too late that the well also housed Popa's corpse.

It all happened so fast. Popa rose from the darkness and grabbed the priest's shoulders. Parnell's feet lifted off the ground as if on their own, like the desks taking flight. Something invisible gave him a nudge. With no way to anchor himself, Popa easily pulled the priest into the hole.

As soon as Parnell tipped over the edge, Popa vanished. The priest struck one side of the well, bounced off, and struck the opposite side before dropping in a freefall. The drop went on seemingly forever.

Splash!

The same water that saved him also threatened to drown him. Screaming when he landed, Parnell had swallowed water right before needing to hold his breath. The water he took in wanted out, and he fought not to cough. Otherwise, he would take in more water and drown. The fall left him disoriented, unable to tell which way was up.

Red striations matching those from the hellish landscape glowed in the near distance. Fire burning in brimstone. Red lines ran like veins across the bottom of the well. The red glow illuminated a series of skeletons in re-pose. The horrific sight informed him which way to swim.

Lungs threatening to burst, and his soaked sacramental clothes threatening to drag him further into the depths, Parnell kicked for the surface, silently praying to God to give him strength. In the flickering surface above, he finally saw a circular light. The well's egress loomed high over-head, too far to reach, but he only needed to get so far to breathe once again.

Parnell surfaced, gasped for much needed breath. He barely took in air when something grabbed his leg or caught it. Either way, it pulled him under. All the way back down. The heat boiled the water near the well's bottom. The striations glowed brighter, lighting up an entrance to a world Parnell wanted no part of. He kicked free of whatever held him and swam until resurfacing again. He spit out water, fought to breathe.

"Help! Camelia, help!"

He would not last. The dual plunges sapped all his strength. The same clothing that brought him closer to God weighed him down. Remaining afloat proved a strug-gle. It would be easy to succumb, to give into the water's embrace. But the boys remained unaccounted for. For them, he would hang on. He rolled over onto his back and did his best to float. The sky above teased him, a heaven out of reach. A land of trees, mountains, and water meant to nourish, not drown.

With a loud splash, a head broke the surface nearby, followed by another, and another. The boys were all in the well. Christian surfaced among them and pointed to the mouth of the well high above.

"It is too far," the priest said.

"Teach us," Christian said.

"Teach us, teach us," the boys chanted in unison.

As wide as the well was, it had grown crowded with so many children. Parnell swam to one side of the well and found a stone outcropping that lined the circumference of the well at roughly water level. Such an outcropping was there for a reason, perhaps for cleaning crews to work from. For the priest, it was a ridge of hope. Parnell gripped the small ledge and braced himself. He called out over his shoulder.

"The light. You boys must go to the light."

And they did. Each climbed onto the priest's shoulders and scrambled up out of his view. He stared straight ahead at stone, fighting not to fall back underwater. The kids were young, they could climb. The entire class rose from the water and stepped onto their teacher's (their new teacher) shoulders.

Parnell noted how the boys felt corporeal. Every scramble of childish hands and limbs awkwardly ascended until they kicked away from the man. Braced as he was, he could not watch their flight. That each climbed atop him in succession meant they had found a way, somehow, to climb. But the priest grew weary. His strength faded.

While he could not look up from where he was, he could look down. Movement caught his eye. Like a shark fin cutting through water, twin dark objects broke the surface and circled off to one side. (Horns?) Parnell yelled.

"Go, now! You must hurry! I can't hold you up for much longer."

The water grew cold enough that Parnell considered revisiting the lower depths where it was warm. The priest shook off the thought. It was a false warmth below. Evil tempted him even in his last moments. Unable to hold on any longer, Parnell slipped away from the wall, drifting toward the center of the well.

Before he could sink into the dark, a hand gripped his. Christian. The boy reached out from above. Christian stood propped on a chain of boys. They stood on one another's shoulders, leading all the way to the top of the well. Christian gestured toward the sky with his head.

The boy helped pull Parnell from the water. Despite his fatigue, the priest found renewed strength in the face of hope. The largest boy stood on the same small rock outcrop that Parnell had clung to. A miracle the child had a spot to plant his feet.

It seemed impossible the boys could hold their ladder-like position, but they never wavered as Parnell climbed over each child, assuring them they were next. Christian climbed close behind the priest.

When Parnell glanced back to check on Christian's progress, the ram horns in the water splashed into the open. Popa, or some twisted version of the man, burst from the water with a face flashing back and forth from that of the professor's original appearance and that of a horned beast. Popa leaped onto the back of the first child in the chain. If the ladder of children was good enough for Parnell, it was good enough for Popa. The sound of fingernails on the chalkboard filled the tight confines of the well. The sound caused the boys to cry out, causing the chain to wobble.

The boys could not hold on to one another and cover their ears. They had to either suffer through the pain or hold steady. Parnell finally reached the top of the well just as the boys began rocking back and forth, losing their strength.

Parnell pulled himself out, finally back on level ground. He wanted nothing more than to drop to the ground and recover, but there was too much at stake. He leaned over the stones and reached for Christian. The stacked boys wavered like scaffolding about to give.

Christian flailed, about to fall back into the well until Parnell grabbed his hand. Parnell had the boy pulled halfway free of the well when Popa grabbed Christian's feet. The boy fell away from the other children and dangled over the edge.

Popa pulled himself up onto Christian's back. Their combined weight was too much for the priest, who struggled not to drop the boy. But Popa was climbing over Christian. If Parnell did not let go, Popa would soon be free of the well.

"No more!" Camelia cried.

She leaned over Parnell's shoulder and splashed holy water on Popa's face.

Popa's face blistered and burned before revealing its true form. The thing that was Popa became a ram with a snout and tusks. The creature's clawed hands slashed Parnell's arms, slicing through his wet clothes like paper. Pain and blood bloomed, but the priest refused to let go of Christian.

Sister Camelia grabbed the loose two-by-four attached to the well and pulled it free. Raising it (and its three nails at its head) as a club, she swung. The nails punctured one of Popa's fiery eyes. Liquid as bright as flowing lava squirted from the creature's orbital socket and the beast let go, falling back into the depths.

Once Popa fell, the shift in weight caused the priest to stumble backward with Christian still in his arms. Parnell fell onto his back, embracing the boy. Exhausted from the struggle, he remained on the ground, trying to regain his strength. The boy on his chest did the same. Two warriors recovering from battle.

The climb had taken so much out of him that Parnell fought to remain conscious. He wanted to rise and help the sister but could not find the strength. But she had her own. Camelia cried out for the boys to hurry. One by one, the students climbed out of the well, somehow using one another as ropes and ladders. Larger boys helped smaller as they all scrambled free. A classroom of students finally graduating.

The priest felt a shift in Christian's body, and the embrace gave way to something less substantial. Christian's skin fluttered away in a mountain breeze. Parnell thought he heard the woods whisper 'thank you' before the boy became nothing but bones. The petite skeleton collapsed under the priest's grip.

As Parnell rose, Christian's skeleton tumbled to the ground in a pile. Other sets of bones lined the perimeter of the well, five in total. Though a classroom full of boys had escaped, only the bones of those originally trapped in the well remained on the ground. Except for Popa, all the well's drowning victims were accounted for. After a brief rest, Parnell and Camelia gave the boys a proper burial.

The nun and priest worked mostly in silence. The weight of what they had accomplished and what they still had to do overwhelmed them. For a time, they were no longer priest and nun, but workers, ditch diggers, just people doing their best to right a tragedy.

Once they buried the boys, Parnell performed a ceremony to bless the water, making the entire well holy water. With everything finished, Camelia wept tears of relief. For so long, she had fought to help the boys and now they were free. But there was only one way to know for certain.

At the break of dawn, both brought chairs to the playground. They sat and waited for hours. When the bell failed to ring at its customary time, the priest and nun gripped hands and celebrated with silence. Class was officially dismissed. The nun and priest were foot soldiers, and they had won the battle.

There was nothing left to do but wait and observe. Boys were precocious. If they were still present, they would not hide for long. But the orphanage remained silent other than the return of birds chirping across the mountainside. Willing to wait as long as it took to be sure, the pair remained seated, watching the shadows where the boys used to play.

About the Author

Paul Carro is an active Horror Writers Association member and author of the acclaimed horror novels *The House* and *Abject Fear*. His short stories have appeared in multiple anthologies. He is editor and coauthor on The Little Coffee Shop of Horrors Anthology series. His screenplay *Penance* is set up with legendary film producer Michael Phillips. He is currently in development on the film and novel adaptation of *Hitchcock, Nebraska* as writer/producer. Horror flick director Rolfe Kanefsky is attached to direct. Paul has served as a producer/writer in film and reality TV, and resides in Santa Monica, California. When not writing Paul is hiking throughout the state.

ALSO BY PAUL CARRO

Scientists trying to cure fear must face their own when the groundbreaking experiment goes horribly wrong. In the race to cure fear there will be casualties. And blood. Lots of blood. Are you ready to face your fears?

"the horror sequences are delightfully grotesque...
" —Kirkus
"Carro blends a conventional horror tale with an innovative, new concept... character backstories are incredible... intriguing and gory." --EbookFairs

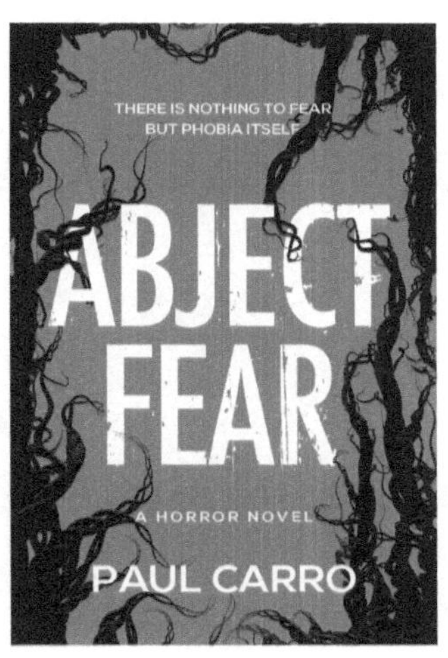

THERE IS NOTHING TO FEAR
BUT PHOBIA ITSELF
ABJECT
FEAR
A HORROR NOVEL
PAUL CARRO

Also by Paul Carro

The day began when Sheriff Frank Watkins discovered two bodies and three heads. Then things got strange. When a mysterious house appears form thin air in a field, the town of Tether Falls, Maine will never be the same. Doors open throughout town and people are transported into a terrifying world beyond their understanding. Soon residents find themselves trapped together. Nine strangers with nine secrets so dark they wish to take them to their graves. One house is willing to accommodate them all. Strap in for a pulse pounding horror thrill ride from acclaimed horror author Paul Carro. A member of the Horror Writers Association, Paul has created a terrifying world where nothing is at it seems. The House is now open. Enter if you dare!

THE
HOUSE
A HORROR NOVEL
PAUL CARRO

Also by Paul Carro

2 authors from 1 family visited 12 coffeeshops to craft 12 single sourced cups of terror!

Authors Paul and Joseph Carro the only known uncle/nephew horror writing duo visited twelve coffeeshops around the country and used the location to inspire twelve unique tales of terror. Each story is prefaced by the coffee shop we worked in and what inspired us. Volume two even adds drink recommendations. If you love naked zombies. killer hill people, and aquatic horror, you will love The Little Coffee Shop of Horrors Anthology. Volumes 1 and 2 available now!

PAUL CARRO
JOSEPH CARRO
WHERE THE SHAKING IS NOT FROM CAFFEINE
BUT FROM THE TWELVE TALES OF TERROR
THE LITTLE
COFFEE SHOP
OF HORRORS
ANTHOLOGY

www.ingramcontent.com/pod-product-compliance
Lightning Source LLC
Chambersburg PA
CBHW031007210726

48290CB00007B/2516